HELEN V. GRIFFITH
More Alex and the Cat

pictures by
DONALD CARRICK

GREENWILLOW BOOKS · New York

FOR PHYLLIS

Text copyright © 1983 by Helen V. Griffith
Illustrations copyright © 1983 by Donald Carrick
All rights reserved. No part of this book
may be reproduced or utilized in any form
or by any means, electronic or mechanical,
including photocopying, recording or by any
information storage and retrieval system,
without permission in writing from the
Publisher, Greenwillow Books, a division
of William Morrow & Company, Inc.
105 Madison Avenue, New York, N.Y. 10016.
Printed in the United States of America
First Edition 10 9 8 7 6 5 4 3 2 1

Library of Congress Cataloging in Publication Data
Griffith, Helen V.
More Alex and the cat.
Summary: The cat teaches Alex the dog
a few more lessons and vice versa.
[1. Cats — Fiction.   2. Dogs — Fiction]
I. Carrick, Donald, ill.   II. Title.
PZ7.G8823Mo 1983   [E]   83-1411
ISBN 0-688-02292-8
ISBN 0-688-02293-6

Contents

Alex's Bone

Alex was digging in the flower bed.
"Did you ever bury a bone and then
forget where?" he asked the cat.
"Never," said the cat.
"That's amazing," said Alex.
He dug up a marigold.
"Oops," he said.

He dug up a petunia.
"Oops," he said. "How do you
remember where you bury your
bones?" he asked the cat.
"Cats don't bury bones," said the cat.

"You just told me that you always find
  your bones," said Alex.
"I didn't say that," said the cat.
"Are you sure?" asked Alex.
"You should listen better," said the cat.

Alex went back to his digging.
"I'd like to find my bone before Robbie
comes out to play," he said.

"School started today," said the cat.

"Robbie's at school."

"Robbie doesn't need school. He knows everything," said Alex.

"Children go to school for years," said the cat.

"Years!" said Alex. He threw himself on
the ground and began to yip. "I want
Robbie!" he yipped.

"He'll be back," said the cat.

"But not for years!" yipped Alex.

"Robbie will be home this afternoon,"
said the cat.

Alex stopped yipping and sat up.

"Really?" he asked.

"Of course," said the cat.

"Then why did you tell me that he would be away for years?" asked Alex.

"I didn't say that," said the cat.

"Are you sure?" asked Alex.

"You should listen better," said the cat.

14

Alex started to dig again. He dug up another petunia. "If I don't find my bone soon," he said, "there won't be any flowers left."

"Eat a biscuit instead," said the cat.

"I'm not hungry," said Alex.

"Then why are you digging up your bone?" asked the cat.

"I'm not digging up my bone," said Alex.

The cat blinked. "You have been talking all morning," he said, "about digging up your bone."
"I'm just looking for it," said Alex.

"Oh," said the cat.

"I'd like to know where it is," said Alex.

"I see," said the cat.

"I don't want to dig it up," said Alex.

"Of course not," said the cat.

"You should listen better," said Alex.

"I should listen less," said the cat.

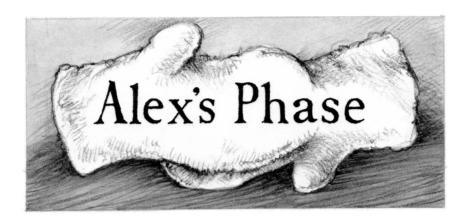

Alex's Phase

Alex was in the yard chewing a mitten.

"Rrrr," he growled.

"Have you seen my pillow?" asked the cat.

"Rrrr," growled Alex.

Robbie came outside.

"Alex!" he yelled. "You're doing it again!"

He grabbed the mitten and held it up.

"It's ruined," he said.

He went back into the house, carrying
the mitten.
Alex's ears drooped. "I hate myself,"
he said.

"Have you seen my pillow?" asked the cat.

"I'm miserable," said Alex.

"About my pillow?" asked the cat.

"About my chewing. I can't stop
  chewing," said Alex.

"Oh," said the cat. He peered under
  a bush. "What could happen
  to a pillow?" he asked.

The cat looked behind a tree. He
crawled under the porch.
"I chew everything," said Alex.
"Magazines and toys and pillows—"
The cat looked out from under the
porch. "Pillows?" he asked.

"And slippers," said Alex, "and furniture and—"

"Did you say pillows?" asked the cat.

"I just can't help myself," said Alex.

The cat crawled out from under the porch.

"You're going through a phase," he said.

"A phase?" asked Alex.

"You'll get over it," said the cat.

"When?" asked Alex.

"Eventually," said the cat.

Alex thought it over. "I used to bark a
lot. That was probably a phase," he said.
"Probably," said the cat.
"Now I only bark when it's important,"
said Alex.
"Hmmm," said the cat.

Robbie opened the door. "Here's your
pillow, kitty," he said. "Nice and clean."
He dropped it into the cat's basket and
went back inside.

The cat leaped onto the porch and sniffed at the pillow. "I was beginning to think you had chewed it up," he said. "So was I," said Alex.

The cat jumped into his basket. He
rolled on his pillow and purred.
Alex sat and watched.

"You know," he said, "I don't feel like
  chewing anymore."
"That's good," purred the cat.

"I think I'm entering a new phase,"
  said Alex.
"That's nice," purred the cat.
"A cat-chasing phase," said Alex.

The cat stopped purring. He looked at
Alex over the side of the basket.
"I can't help myself," Alex shouted.
He ran up the porch steps. He pranced
around the cat, barking and growling.

The cat stood up. He arched his back
and hissed. His fur stuck out all over.
Alex stopped prancing and barking.
He sat down and wagged his tail.
"Some phases are very short," he said.

The cat smoothed his fur. He settled
himself in his basket and watched Alex
over the side. Alex picked up a mitten
and began to chew.

"You're doing it again," said the cat.

"Rrrr," growled Alex.

"I thought you were tired of chewing," said the cat.

"I am," said Alex.

"Then why are you chewing the other mitten?" asked the cat.

"Oh, well," said Alex, "what good is one mitten?"

Alex and the Cold Air

"I hate winter," Alex told the cat.
"What's wrong with winter?" asked
the cat.
"Everything," said Alex. "Robbie has
school, it gets dark early, and the cold
air chaps my nose."

"The air chaps your nose?" asked the cat.

"Yes," said Alex. "Look. And it's only November."

"Maybe you should hibernate," said the cat.

"What's hibernate?" asked Alex.

"Sleep through the winter," said the cat.

"Like bears do?" asked Alex.

"That's the idea," said the cat.

Alex thought it over. "It's worth a try,"
he said.
He dug down into a pile of leaves.
He curled himself into a tight ball
and lay very still.

An ant crawled across his paw. Leaves tickled his nose. He began to itch all over.

All at once he jumped up and shook
the leaves off his back. "Bears must not
be ticklish," he said.
"That could be true," said the cat.
Alex tried to look at his nose. "I think
it's worse," he said, "and it's still only
November."

"Maybe you should migrate," said
   the cat.
"What's migrate?" asked Alex.
"Go south," said the cat, "where it's
   warm."
"Like birds do?" asked Alex.
"That's the idea," said the cat.
"It's worth a try," said Alex. "Which
   way is south?"

Just then a cold wind blew across the
yard. There were snowflakes in it. They
fell on Alex and the cat. They began
to cover the ground.

"Snow!" said Alex. He let a snowflake
land on his tongue. "I love snow," he said.
"Doesn't it chap your nose?" asked the cat.
"Who cares?" said Alex.

He jumped up and caught a snowflake in
his mouth.
"Aren't you going to migrate?" asked the cat.
"What, and leave this snow?" asked Alex.

He leaped into the air, snapping at
snowflakes. He ran through the yard,
pouncing on snowflakes.

"Come and play," he called to the cat.
The cat hunched his back and tucked
his paws into his fur. "No, thanks,"
he said.
"It's snowing harder," called Alex.
"How nice," said the cat.

"And just think," Alex said with a leap
and a pounce, "it's only November!"

Helen V. Griffith is the author of *Alex and the Cat,* which
was chosen by *School Library Journal* as a Best Book
of Spring 1982, *Alex Remembers,* and *Mine Will, Said John.*
She grew up in Delaware, where she still lives, and works
in her family's roofing and siding business. She is
an ardent birdwatcher who uses her vacations to add new
species to her list, and her spare time to write books
for young readers.

Donald Carrick is a favorite with picture book fans. He is
the illustrator of *Alex Remembers* by Helen V. Griffith,
and has written and illustrated such highly praised books
as *The Deer in the Pasture* and *Harald and the Giant Knight.*
He has also illustrated, among others, *The Highest Balloon
on the Common, Paul's Christmas Birthday* and *Crocodile
Still Waits* by his wife, Carol Carrick. The Carricks
and their two children live on Martha's Vineyard, and all
spend their summers in Vermont.

DATE DUE